Michael Bird-Boy

TOMIE dePAOLA

SIMON & SCHUSTER BOOKS FOR YOUNG READERS

NEW YORK   LONDON   TORONTO   SYDNEY   NEW DELHI

To Boss-Lady

SIMON & SCHUSTER BOOKS FOR YOUNG READERS
An imprint of Simon & Schuster Children's Publishing Division
1230 Avenue of the Americas, New York, New York 10020
Copyright © 1975 by Tomie dePaola
All rights reserved, including the right of reproduction in whole or in part in any form.
SIMON & SCHUSTER BOOKS FOR YOUNG READERS is a trademark of Simon & Schuster, Inc.
For information about special discounts for bulk purchases, please contact Simon & Schuster Special Sales
at 1-866-506-1949 or business@simonandschuster.com.
The Simon & Schuster Speakers Bureau can bring authors to your live event. For more information or to book an event,
contact the Simon & Schuster Speakers Bureau at 1-866-248-3049 or visit our website at www.simonspeakers.com.
Book design by Laurent Linn
The text for this book is set in Alghera Std.
The illustrations for this book are rendered in watercolor, colored pencil, and ink on Fabriano 150lb Artistico paper.
Manufactured in China
0715 SCP
This Simon & Schuster Books for Young Readers hardcover edition October 2015
2 4 6 8 10 9 7 5 3 1
Library of Congress Cataloging-in-Publication Data
DePaola, Tomie, 1934- author, illustrator.
Michael bird-boy / story and pictures by Tomie dePaola.
pages cm
Originally published: Englewood Cliffs, New Jersey : Prentice-Hall, 1975.
Summary: A young boy who loves the countryside determines to find the source of the black cloud that hovers above it.
ISBN 978-1-4814-4333-3 (hardcover) — ISBN 978-1-4814-4555-9 (ebook) [1. Air—Pollution—Fiction.
2. Nature—Effect of human beings on—Fiction.] I. Title.
PZ7.D439Mi 2015
[E]—dc23
2014040100

Michael Bird-Boy lived in the country.

Every day was the same. He woke up and washed his face.

He put on his bird suit and ate his breakfast.

Then Michael Bird-Boy did his work. At night, he sat down and looked at the stars.

And every day was different.

The sky and the leaves were always different.

But one day was very different. A black cloud came across the sky.

And when night came, Michael Bird-Boy couldn't see the moon
or the stars.

The white birds were dirty. The flowers wilted.

So he packed his suitcase

and went off to find what was causing the black cloud.

He walked and walked until he came to the city.

And there he saw it.

"Hi, I'm Boss-Lady," said a voice.

"I'm Michael Bird-Boy," said Michael. "Your factory is making the countryside very dark and dirty."

"I'm sorry, Mike," said Boss-Lady. "I make Genuine Shoe-Fly Artificial Honey Syrup in my factory. It's great on pancakes. But melting all that sugar in the big furnace makes a lot of black smoke."

"Why don't you make real honey?" asked Michael Bird-Boy. "Bees don't make smoke."

"Where can I get some bees?" asked Boss-Lady.

"I'll send you some," said Michael Bird-Boy.

So Michael Bird-Boy went back to the country and sent Boss-Lady
some bees. She shut off her furnace and started to make real honey.

The white birds were white again, the flowers weren't wilted anymore, and Michael Bird-Boy could see the stars and moon at night.

One day the telephone rang. "Hello, Mike, this is Boss-Lady.
I have a terrible problem. Your bees aren't working."

So Michael Bird-Boy went all the way back to Boss-Lady's factory.
She was waiting for him. "Come inside," she said.

"Look! No honey!" she said, pointing to the rows of empty jars.
"The bees are just sitting there buzzing!"

"I planned it so carefully," she said. "Look at my charts!"

Michael Bird-Boy looked.

"Where are the flowers?" he asked.

"Flowers?" said Boss-Lady.

"Bees need flowers and hives," said Michael Bird-Boy.

And he drew a picture to show Boss-Lady how bees make honey.
"No wonder no honey," said Boss-Lady. "Thanks again, Mike."

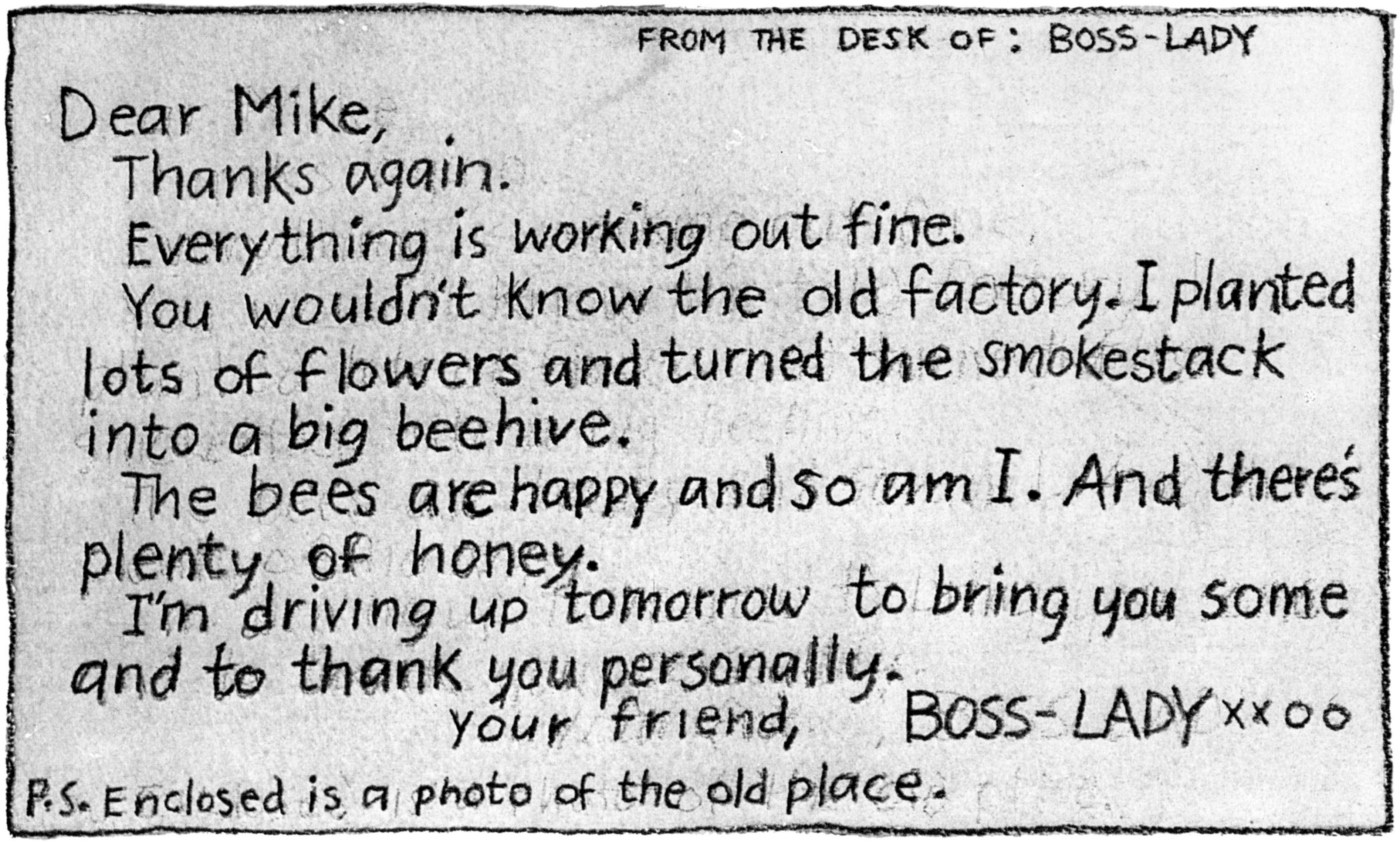
FROM THE DESK OF: BOSS-LADY

Dear Mike,

Thanks again.

Everything is working out fine.

You wouldn't know the old factory. I planted lots of flowers and turned the smokestack into a big beehive.

The bees are happy and so am I. And there's plenty of honey.

I'm driving up tomorrow to bring you some and to thank you personally.

your friend, BOSS-LADY xxoo

P.S. Enclosed is a photo of the old place.

A few weeks later Michael Bird-Boy got a letter.

The next day Boss-Lady arrived in her pickup loaded with honey.
"Oh good!" said Michael Bird-Boy. "I'll bake us a honey cake."

And he did, while Boss-Lady told him all the details.

Then they had a party.

And that night Michael Bird-Boy and Boss-Lady sat among the flowers
with the white birds and watched the annual comet display.

Good night.